Walking through the Jungle

Barefoot Books
124 Walcot Street
Bath BA1 5BG, UK

Barefoot Books
2067 Massachusetts Ave
Cambridge, MA 02140, USA

First published in Great Britain by Barefoot Books, Ltd and in the United States of America by Barefoot Books, Inc. in 1997
This paperback edition published in 2006

This book has been printed on 100% acid-free paper

Graphic design by Tom Grzelinski, Bath, England
Printed and bound by Printplus Ltd, China

The Library of Congress has cataloged the first paperback edition as follows:

Harter, Debbie.
Walking through the jungle / [written and] illustrated by Debbie Harter.
p. cm.
Summary: A young explorer discovers the different animals and terrains or the world before making it home,
safe and sound, for supper.
ISBN 1-84148-182-3 (pbk. with cd : alk. paper)
[1. Animals-Fiction. 2. Stories in rhyme.] I. Title.
PZ8.3.H257Wal 2004
[E]--dc22

2004010525

Paperback ISBN 1-905236-99-9

British Cataloguing-in-Publication Data:
a catalogue record for this book is available from the British Library

5 7 9 8 6 4

Walking through the Jungle

Illustrated by Debbie Harter

Barefoot Books
Celebrating Art and Story

Walking through the jungle,
Walking through the jungle,

What do you see?
What do you see?

Chasing after me,
Chasing after me.

What do you see?
What do you see?

I think I see a whale,

Whoo

Whoos

Whoosh

Chasing after me,
Chasing after me.

Climbing in the mountains,
Climbing in the mountains,

What do you see?
What do you see?

Chasing after me,
Chasing after me.

Swimming in the river,
Swimming in the river,

What do you see?
What do you see?

Chasing after me,
Chasing after me.

Trekking in the desert,
Trekking in the desert,

What do you see?
What do you see?

Chasing after me,
Chasing after me.

Slipping on the iceberg,
Slipping on the iceberg,

What do you see?
What do you see?

I think I see a polar bear,

Growl! Growl! Growl!

Chasing after me,
Chasing after me.

Running home for supper,
Running home for supper,

Where have you been?
Where have you been?

I've been around the world and back,
I've been around the world and back,

And guess what I've seen,
And guess what I've seen.